Hurry Up!
Hurry Up!
¡Deprisa! ¡Deprisa!

by Deborah Schecter

ISBN: 978-1-338-70295-8
Illustrated by Anne Kennedy
Copyright © 2020 by Deborah Schecter. All rights reserved.
Published by Scholastic Inc., 557 Broadway, New York, NY 10012

10 9 8 7 6   68   23 24 25 26/0

Printed in Jiaxing, China. First printing, June 2020.

SCHOLASTIC

Get out of bed.
Hurry up! Hurry up!

Me levanto.
¡Deprisa! ¡Deprisa!

Brush my teeth.
Hurry up! Hurry up!

Me lavo los dientes.
¡Deprisa! ¡Deprisa!

Get dressed.
Hurry up! Hurry up!

Me visto.
¡Deprisa! ¡Deprisa!

Eat breakfast.
Hurry up! Hurry up!

Desayuno.
¡Deprisa! ¡Deprisa!

Take my lunch.
Hurry up! Hurry up!

Agarro el almuerzo.
¡Deprisa! ¡Deprisa!

Get the bus.
Hurry up! Hurry up!

Tomo el autobús.
¡Deprisa! ¡Deprisa!

It is the first day of school!
Hurry up! Hurry up!

¡Es el primer día de escuela!
¡Deprisa! ¡Deprisa!